Daisy Dawson

and the Secret Pool

Other Racing Reads:

Daisy Dawson

Daisy Dawson and the Secret Pool

Daisy Dawson and the Big Freeze

Daisy Dawson at the Seaside

Daisy Dawson on the Farm

by Steve Voake

The No. 1 Car Spotter

The No. 1 Car Spotter and the Firebird

The No. 1 Car Spotter and the Car Thieves

by Atinuke

Anna Hibiscus

Hooray for Anna Hibiscus!

Good Luck, Anna Hibiscus!

Have Fun, Anna Hibiscus!

Welcome Home, Anna Hibiscus!

Go Well, Anna Hibiscus!

by Atinuke

Steve Voake

illustrated by Jessica Meserve

WALKER
BOOKS

This is a work of fiction. Names, characters, places and incidents are either the product of the author's imagination or, if real, used fictitiously. All statements, activities, stunts, descriptions, information and material of any other kind contained herein are included for entertainment purposes only and should not be relied on for accuracy or replicated as they may result in injury.

First published 2008 by Walker Books Ltd
87 Vauxhall Walk, London SE11 5HJ

8 10 9 7

This book has been typeset in StempelSchneidler

Printed and bound in Great Britain by Clays Ltd, St Ives plc

British Library Cataloguing in Publication Data:
a catalogue record for this book is available from the British Library

ISBN 978-1-4063-0401-5

www.walker.co.uk

For Daisy Voake, with love

S.V.

For Emily

J.M.

Wasps and Chocolate

"Smile, please!" said Daisy as she pressed the button and a bright flash lit up the bathroom. Her Dad's foam-covered face froze in the viewfinder, razor held in mid-air and eyebrows raised in surprise.

"Hey!" he protested, scraping another pathway through the foam. "If I'd known we were doing a photo shoot, I'd have ironed my boxer shorts."

Daisy reversed into the bedroom, fell backwards onto the double bed and took an action shot of the ceiling on her way down.

"Hey!" said Mum, lifting her teacup out of harm's way. "Mind where you're bouncing, missus!"

"Sorry," said Daisy. "But a good photographer has to be able to take photos on the move." (She had read this in a magazine at the dentist's, so she knew it was true.)

"Pleased with the new camera, then?" asked Dad, towelling his face dry.

"Best birthday present ever," said Daisy. She turned around to take a snap of her mum drinking her tea.

"Well don't waste the film," said Mum, as she flicked through her magazine. "I'm not sure the world is ready for pictures of your dad in his boxer shorts."

"Thousands would disagree," said Dad.

"Don't worry," said Daisy. "It's digital. See? You can just wipe it off if you don't like it." She pressed a button and the picture

dissolved away
to nothing. "There,"
she said. "All gone!"

Daisy's mum looked
at the clock, then dropped her
magazine and sprang out of bed. "Gone is
where we all should be. It's a quarter past
eight already!"

* * *

Daisy put her camera back on the shelf and hoped she wouldn't be late for school again. Miss Frink had suggested setting her alarm clock ten minutes earlier, but this just meant she had more time to do interesting things before she left the house.

She picked up the bottle of Strawberry Surprise (birthday perfume from Grandma) and squirted some under her chin.
It reminded her of those delicious chewy red sweets she liked so much, so she gave herself another quick blast. Then she swung her satchel over her shoulder, jumped down the stairs three at a time and ambled into the kitchen.

"Poo–ee," said Dad. "What's that smell?"

"It's my perfume," replied Daisy.
"Strawberry Surprise."

"Surprise is right," said Dad, wrinkling up his nose.

"Come on, Daisy," said Mum. "Stop faffing about and get your skates on. You know what Miss Frink said about you being late."

"Don't worry, Mum," said Daisy, kissing her on the cheek and skipping out of the back door. "Daisy Dawson is on her way!"

* * *

Daisy wandered down the lane listening to the bees buzz and the swallows sing. Apart from a few bumpy white clouds here and there, the sky was clean and empty. With the sun warming her face, Daisy leant on the gate and gazed at the old tumble-down barn.

"Boom!" she called. "I've brought you some breakfast!"

There was a scrabbling sound from inside the barn and a large bloodhound poked its head through a hole in the wall.

"Morning, Daisy," he said. "You're bright and early."

"Well I *was*," replied Daisy as Boom lumbered towards her. "But I got involved in a photo shoot, so..."

It was only a few weeks since Daisy's encounter with the magical yellow butterfly, but she was already so used to talking to animals that it didn't seem in the least bit strange to her. In fact, it would have seemed stranger if she'd suddenly discovered she *couldn't* talk to them.

"A photo shoot?" asked Boom. "What's one of those?"

"I got a new camera for my birthday and I've been taking photos with it," said Daisy. Boom looked puzzled, so she tried to explain. "You know when you shut your eyes and, if you concentrate, you can still see someone's face for a while?"

Boom shut his eyes and nodded.

"Well," said Daisy, "a camera stops it from fading away. I'll show you tomorrow, if you like."

"I *would* like," said Boom. Then he sniffed the air. "Have you been making jam sandwiches?"

"Oh, that'll be my new perfume," said Daisy. "Strawberry Surprise." She opened her lunchbox and took out the ham sandwich she had made for him. "Would you prefer jam tomorrow?"

"No thanks," replied Boom, chomping on the sandwich. "Jam is fine, but ham is *divine*. Want some company?"

"Always," said Daisy. She opened the gate to let him out and together they trotted off down the lane.

"BUZZY-BUZZY JAM JAM
BUZZY-BUZZY JAM JAM
ME-WANT ME-WANT ME-WANT ME-WANT!
BUZZY-BUZZY JAM JAM
BUZZY-BUZZY JAM JAM
ME-WANT ME-WANT ME-WANT ME-WANT!"

"Aargh!" squealed Daisy, flapping her arms about. "It's a wasp!"

"BUZZY-BUZZY JAM JAM
BUZZY-BUZZY JAM JAM
ME-WANT ME-WANT ME-WANT ME-WANT!"

"Keep still," said Boom as the wasp circled above Daisy's head. "He'll fly away in a minute."

"But he's not flying away!" squeaked Daisy. "He keeps trying to land on me!"

"I expect it's your perfume," said Boom. "Tell him."

"What?" asked Daisy, flapping frantically. "What d'you mean, 'tell him'?"

"Just tell him he's wasting his time," said Boom.

"Oh," said Daisy. She fixed the wasp with a hard stare. "Now listen here," she said sternly. "I haven't got anything for you to eat, so why don't you just buzz off?"

The wasp flew back a little way and hovered in front of her.

"BUZZY-WHAT? BUZZY-WHAT? BUZZY-WHAT? BUZZY-WHAT?"

"I'm *saying*," said Daisy, "that whatever you want, I haven't got it."

"FIBBER-BUZZ
FIBBER-BUZZ
FIBBER-BUZZ
FIB!"

"I am *not* a fibber," said Daisy irritably. "What you can smell is my strawberry perfume, that's all. You can't eat it, so you might as well leave me alone and go and do something useful instead."

"That'll be the day," said Boom.

The wasp changed direction and began buzzing angrily around Boom's head.

Boom yawned. "Why don't you just calm down for a minute and listen to what she's trying to tell you?"

The wasp settled on a fence post.

"BUT I'M SMELLIN' IT, I'M SMELLIN' IT, I'M SMELLIN' IT, I'M *SMELLIN'* IT!"

"I told you," Daisy explained, "it's my perfume. You *can't* eat it."

The wasp crawled around on top of the fence post, buzzing its wings impatiently.

"DON'T CARE, DON'T CARE, WANNIT, WANNIT, WANNIT, WANNIT!"

"I tell you what," said Daisy, taking out her lunchbox. "I'll let you have a bit of my chocolate biscuit if you promise to leave me alone."

"GIVE IT-WANNIT-GIVE IT-WANNIT-GIVE IT-WANNIT-GIVE IT-WANNIT!"

"I think," said Boom, "that's as close as you're going to get."

"All right," said Daisy, putting a small piece of chocolate on top of the fence post. "But a deal's a deal, remember."

"BUZZY-NUMMY, BUZZY-NUMMY, BUZZY-NUMMY, NUM-NUM!"

"I think he likes it," said Daisy as they walked away. "He was a bit rude though, wasn't he? Not very well brought up."

"Ah," said Boom, "but think about that poor queen, having to lay eggs all day long. If you were a single mum with ten thousand kids, would you have time to teach them any manners?"

"That," said Daisy thoughtfully, "is a very good point."

Somewhere in the distance, a bell rang.

"Uh-oh. Speaking of chocolate, I think I'm going to be the end of it."

"Eh?" said Boom.

Daisy smiled. "Chock-oh-*late*."

She hitched up her satchel, kissed the top of his head and ran off down the lane.

Boom watched her go for a few moments, then sat and stared at a small snail.

"I don't get it," he said.

Late Again

When she reached her classroom, Daisy peered through a crack in the door and saw that Miss Frink's pen was poised above the register. Why couldn't she have been called Daisy *Zinkleman*? At least then she'd have a chance of making it to her seat on time.

As it was, Miss Frink had done Kimberly Kibble and was already galloping flat out towards Gareth Watkins and Abigail Wilson. To make matters worse it was Quiet Reading Time, and unless

Bobby Mitchell fell off his chair into the display of junk models ("We Have Been Designing Our Own Houses") there was no way she would make it in unnoticed.

"Four legs, please, Bobby," said Miss Frink, removing Daisy's last hope. "And that doesn't include your own."

As Bobby's chair thumped back onto the carpet, Daisy opened the door and strode quickly across to her place, hoping that no one would notice.

"Good morning, Daisy," snapped Miss Frink. "Or should I say *good afternoon*?"

Oh dear, thought Daisy. Rumbled again.

"Good morning, Miss Frink," she said, hooking her satchel over the back of her chair. Jessica Jenkins beamed at her from the next table, but as Daisy smiled back, Miss Frink said, "I hope you don't think this is funny, Daisy Dawson."

"No, Miss Frink," said Daisy. "I don't

think it's funny."

"Well I do," said Furball the gerbil through the bars of his cage. "I Frink it's hilarious, actually."

"Stop it," Daisy told him sternly.

"And it's no good muttering under your breath either," Miss Frink went on. "It's time you pulled your socks up, young lady. Next week, I want you here before the bell goes. Is that clear?"

"Yes, Miss Frink," said Daisy. She sat down and glared at Furball.

"Don't get huffy with me," he said. "I was here in plenty of time."

"Yeah," said Burble, popping her head up next to him. "Like you had a *choice*."

She peered at Daisy through the bars. "All right, Daisy D?"

Daisy nodded and looked in Miss Frink's direction.

"Oh right, got it. No can talk." Burble pretended to zip her mouth shut with her paw. "Catch you later, then."

Daisy gave a thumbs up, then turned back to Miss Frink, who was now standing in front of the class. "All eyes this way, please."

Two little sucking noises came from the gerbils' cage and Daisy saw that Furball was pretending to remove his eyeballs. She decided to ignore him.

"This morning we are going to start our research into habitats," said Miss Frink. "Who can tell me what a habitat is?"

Daisy thrust her hand up into the air, but Bobby Mitchell was there first, supporting his outstretched arm with his free hand and mumbling, "Ooh, ooh!"

"All right Bobby," said Miss Frink. "Enlighten us."

"A habitat," said Bobby, "is a shop where they sell sofas."

Everyone burst out laughing, including Bobby. Although he wasn't sure why he was laughing, he was delighted that his answer had gone down so well.

"Thank you Bobby," said Miss Frink. "Now has anyone got a *sensible* suggestion?"

Puzzled, Bobby leant back on his chair and began chewing the end of his pencil.

"Daisy? Perhaps you can redeem yourself this morning?"

Daisy sat up straight and thought about the video they had watched last term.

"A habitat is a place where animals make their homes," she said.

"Good," said Miss Frink. "Can you give us an example?"

"Well," said Daisy, "rabbits live in fields, so that's their natural habitat and, um, squirrels live up trees, so that's their habitat."

"Splendid," said Miss Frink. "Those are two very good examples, Daisy. Now we are going to read about Different Habitats Around The World. I want you all to make some notes, then later on I'll tell you about your Special Assignment For The Weekend."

The library monitors had made a display of reference books at the side of the classroom and Daisy's table was allowed to go up first and choose.

Daisy found a photograph of some gerbils in a sandy desert and sidled up to Burble and Furball's cage.

"Pssst!" she whispered. "You two! Come and have a look at this!"

The gerbils scampered over and stuck their noses through the bars. Daisy opened the book and showed them the picture.

"Wow!" said Furball. "Excellent!"

"Anyone we know?" asked Burble.

"That's your natural habitat," whispered Daisy. "It's where your ancestors came from."

"No way!" said Burble.

"Cool!" said Furball. "My grandpa was a surf dude!" He began to do a little dance, twisting his feet in the sawdust and singing:

"Surf's up sugar, come 'n' surf it with me!"

Daisy remembered how much he had enjoyed last term's project on the seaside and decided she had better break it to him gently.

"It's not a beach, Furball," she explained. "It's a *desert*."

"Course it's a beach," said Furball, continuing to dance around with his paws held out in front of him as if stirring a large spoon. "Look at all the sand! Imagine that! Running down to the sea every morning, catching a few waves and still making it back for breakfast. Surf-tastic!"

"It would have to be a very late breakfast," said Daisy. "The beach is about a thousand miles away."

"A thousand miles?" exclaimed Furball, stopping his dance. "A thousand *miles*?"

Burble cupped a paw to her ear. "Is it me, or is there an echo in here?"

"Like I said, it's a *desert* habitat," Daisy explained patiently. "That means lots of sun, lots of sand, but no sea."

"Not even a rock pool?" Furball asked hopefully.

Daisy shook her head. "'Fraid not."

"Well I can't see the point of that," said Furball. "I'd rather live here, to be honest."

"That's lucky," said Burble.

"Got any Cheesy Wotsits?" asked Furball, changing the subject.

"I've got some in my lunchbox," said Daisy. "I'll go and get you one."

"One?" said Furball.

"I was right," said Burble. "There is an echo in here."

Hazel and Conker

On her way home from school that afternoon, Daisy saw Meadowsweet grazing in the farmer's field and stopped off to talk to her.

"Hello, my lovely," said Meadowsweet, putting her head over the gate and nuzzling Daisy's hair. "Have you had a nice day at school?"

"Pretty good actually," said Daisy, "although I was late again this morning."

"Oh well," replied Meadowsweet.

"There's no point in rushing, I say. Folks'll always wait if they want you."

Daisy smiled. "I must remember to tell Miss Frink that one."

She climbed the gate and jumped down into the field.

"Hello, Daisy!" called a voice from the old oak tree.

"Hello, Cyril!" Daisy waved at the grey squirrel scampering along the branches and noticed that two smaller squirrels were skipping along behind him.

"Who's Cyril got with him?" she asked.

"That's Hazel and Conker," said Meadowsweet. "They're his sister's children. Cyril's agreed to look after them while she visits friends in Leafscuffle Wood. I think he's beginning to regret it already."

Cyril bounded down the tree trunk and stopped next to the horse trough, closely followed by Hazel and Conker.

"Look!" exclaimed Conker, jumping up onto the edge of the trough. "A swimming pool! Can we go swimming, Uncle Cyril? Can we? Please? Can we?"

"No," said Cyril firmly. "Squirrels don't *go* swimming. Didn't your mother teach you anything?"

"Nope," said Conker cheerfully.

"Does that mean I can go in, then?"

"No," said Cyril. "It does not."

"What if I *fell* in?"

"Accidentally on purpose you mean?" giggled Hazel.

"All right, that's enough," said Cyril. "Come on. Come down off there."

Daisy tried to keep a straight face as Conker held out his arms and walked unsteadily along the side of the trough, like a tightrope walker in a high wind.

"Wibbly wobbly, wibbly wobbly..."

"Conker!" scolded Cyril.

As Conker jumped down and somersaulted across the grass, Daisy noticed that Hazel was staring at her.

"Hello," said Daisy. "You must be Hazel."

"Yes," replied Hazel shyly. "Are you Daisy? Uncle Cyril told us all about the Battle of Krackdown Kennels. About how he was a big brave hero and you helped him a tiny bit..."

"Yes, yes, yes," interrupted Cyril hurriedly. "I'm sure Daisy doesn't want to be reminded of all that again, do you Daisy? I expect you've got some important business to be getting on with, eh?"

"Well actually, I have got a project to do this weekend," said Daisy. "We're supposed to find out about some animal habitats near where we live. I was wondering if I could come and take a few photos tomorrow?"

"Photos?" piped up Conker. "What's photos?"

"You take them with a camera," Daisy explained. "You just go *click-click* and then you've got a picture to keep for ever."

"Don't know what you're on about," replied Conker, "but it sounds brilliant."

"Can I take a picture of *you*, Daisy?" asked Hazel in a small voice.

Daisy crouched down and stroked Hazel's head. "Of course you can."

"Gosh," whispered Hazel. "Thanks, Daisy!" Then she ran around and hid behind Cyril.

At that moment a sleek grey cat emerged from the bushes, settled in a patch of warm sunlight and regarded Daisy with cool green eyes. It was Trixie McDixie.

"So," purred Trixie, "you want to take some pictures."

"Yes," said Daisy. "I thought I'd take some of Cyril and Meadowsweet in their natural habitat."

"Hmm," said Trixie. "Not wishing to be rude of course, but wouldn't you like to take pictures of something a little less … ordinary?"

"Hey!" protested Cyril. "I'm a one-off, I am! I'm unique!"

"Can't argue with that," said Trixie. "Even so."

"What did you have in mind?" asked Daisy.

"Well it just so happens that while I was out hunting in the woods last night, I heard a whisper that a pair of otters have moved in a few miles downriver. They keep themselves to themselves of course, but it might be worth the trip just to get something … how shall I put this … that isn't a squirrel."

"What's *wrong* with squirrels?" demanded Cyril.

"How long have you got?" purred Trixie.

"There's *nothing* wrong with squirrels," said Daisy hurriedly. "But it does sound rather exciting. We could have an expedition."

"An expedition!" exclaimed Cyril, cheering up immediately. "I could be team leader!"

"Oh please," said Trixie. "Give me a break."

"Can we come?" chorused Hazel and Conker. "Can we, can we?"

"I don't know," said Cyril cautiously. "It could be highly dangerous." He looked pointedly in Conker's direction. "A mission such as this would only be suitable for *sensible* squirrels."

Conker immediately stood up straight and put his paws by his sides. "I can do sensible."

Hazel went cross-eyed behind Cyril's back in an attempt to make Conker laugh. Conker sniggered, then stamped his foot and saluted. "Corporal Conker reporting for duty, sah!"

"Look, I can't take any more of this," said Trixie irritably. "If you're interested, Daisy, my advice is to ditch the squirrels and follow the river down past Darkwater Sump. Keep your wits about you and you should be able to find them."

"Wait!" said Daisy as Trixie disappeared into the bushes. "What's Darkwater Sump?"

"Darkwater Sump," said a familiar voice behind her, "is a deep hole which sucks water down beneath the river bed."

"Boom!" Daisy reached out to pat him as he sat down beside her. "Are you coming on our expedition?"

"Of course," said Boom, "but we'll need to be careful. They say Darkwater Sump is a dangerous place for the unwary."

Daisy noticed that Cyril was drawing a sketch map in the dust.

"All right, everyone," he announced. "Gather round!"

As they clustered around the map, Cyril used a twig to point out key objectives.

"Now this," he said, "is our starting point, where we shall assemble at 0900 hours, then proceed down the riverbank in an orderly fashion."

"Looks like a dandelion to me," said Hazel.

“Well it *is* a dandelion,” replied Cyril wearily. “I’m trying to show you where things are, that’s all. That’s the whole point of a map. The dandelion is *irrelevant*.”

“An elephant?” asked Hazel, at which point Conker burst out laughing and had to stuff a dock leaf in his mouth to muffle the sound.

“Look,” snapped Cyril, “are you sure I can trust you to be sensible squirrels?”

“Pleeuhh!” said Conker, spitting out the dock leaf.

“Of course,” said Hazel, stepping in front of him. “We’re always sensible.”

There was silence for a moment, followed by a tremendous splash. As everyone turned to look, Conker stuck his head out of the horse trough and grinned.

“Anyone fancy a swim?”

Daisy's Expedition

Daisy woke up early the next morning and began to pack the things she would need. She picked up her blue rucksack and carefully put in her camera and a clean pair of socks, just in case. Then she found her waterproof at the back of the wardrobe and stuffed it in on top. Although it looked as though it was going to be another bright, sunny day, there were one or two grey clouds on the horizon and the lady on last night's weather forecast had said there could be sudden showers *almost anywhere.*

Daisy had been in the Brownies, so she knew the importance of Being Prepared.

She tiptoed down into the kitchen and made enough supplies to keep her and Boom going through what she guessed would be quite a long day. Extra-thick ham sandwiches, two packets of cheese-and-onion crisps and a couple of chocolate biscuits, plus an extra one in case of emergency.

"Morning, Daisy," said Boom as Daisy climbed over the gate and patted Meadowsweet on the neck. "Reckon we might get wet today."

"D'you think?" asked Daisy, glancing up to see that the number of clouds on the horizon had somehow doubled since the last time she'd looked. But there was still plenty of blue sky around, so she decided there wasn't too much to worry about.

She watched Conker at the top of the tree, dropping acorns into the water trough, while Cyril tried to explain something to a bored-looking Hazel.

"Cyril's getting wet already," Daisy said with a grin.

"I don't mean to hurry you," interrupted Meadowsweet, "but if you're going, it might be best to make an early start."

"Aren't you coming with us?" Daisy asked.

"I'm afraid not," said Meadowsweet. "The path is too narrow for me. But I'll be waiting right here until you're safely home."

Daisy looked round to see Hazel and Conker scampering across the field towards the woods, with Cyril chasing after them shouting, "Wait! I'm the leader! Leader goes first!"

"Be careful, won't you?" said Meadowsweet.

But Daisy and Boom were already running to catch up with the others. Meadowsweet watched them until they reached the edge of the field; two tiny dots beneath a sky that was becoming darker and greyer with every second.

* * *

"This way, everyone!" called Cyril.

Daisy climbed the fence and scrambled down the riverbank. She knelt on sun-dappled stones and splashed cool water on her face. Boom waited patiently, then waded slowly and carefully through the river beside her as she skipped across the stones to the other side.

They followed Cyril along the woodland path, the light tinged with green where sunshine filtered through the leaves.

"Halt!" shouted Cyril suddenly. "Everybody halt!"

Hazel and Conker staged a mini pile-up behind him, knocking Cyril sprawling into a patch of wild garlic.

He leapt to his feet, brushed bark from his coat and, staggering slightly, pointed to a wire fence in front of them.

"That," he warned, "is an electric fence. Whatever you do, do *not* touch it!"

"What's it for?" Daisy whispered.

"It marks the edge of the farmer's land," explained Boom. "Makes sure that any lost sheep don't stray too far from home."

"Look," said Daisy, pointing down the riverbank. "The fence stops at that tree. How about we walk along the river until we get past it?"

"We could," replied Boom, "but the river comes right up to the bank."

"Oh well," said Daisy. "We'll just have to get wet."

"You're forgetting something," said Cyril. "Squirrels can climb trees. In fact, climbing trees is what we do best."

"Of course," said Daisy. "I hadn't thought of that."

She looked up at the big old beech tree and saw that even its lowest branches were too high for her to reach.

"I tell you what," she said. "You squirrels climb the tree and Boom and I will go the river way. Then we'll meet up on the other side."

"Dear me, no!" said Cyril. "That would never do. I couldn't possibly abandon members of my platoon. What if a shark attacked you? How would I live with myself?"

Daisy smiled. "Sharks don't live in rivers. It's not their natural habitat. A shark's natural habitat is the sea."

"Ah," said Cyril knowingly, "but has anyone told *them* that?"

"Well..." said Daisy hesitantly.

Boom shook his head as if he couldn't quite believe what he was hearing.

"I tell you what," said Daisy, "if we see any sharks, we'll call you. Then you can distract them by throwing acorns or something."

At that moment there was a sharp crack and everyone turned around to see Conker lying flat on his back next to the electric fence.

"He touched it! He touched it!" Hazel squealed. "Conker touched the electric fence!"

"Oh *no*!" Daisy exclaimed.

But to everyone's relief Conker got unsteadily to his feet and gave a lop-sided grin, little strands of smoke rising from his fur.

"Woah!" he said, sounding impressed. "That fence kicks like a kangaroo!"

"Oooh, can I have a go?" asked Hazel, jumping up and down with excitement. "Please Uncle Cyril! Can I? Can I?"

Before Cyril could answer there was another loud crack and Conker flew past them into a clump of nettles. He sat up, blinked and rubbed his face. "Ow," he said. "That one was a stinger!"

"Conker, for heaven's sake," said Cyril. "Pack it in!"

"*Please* can I have a go?" begged Hazel.

"No, you most certainly cannot," replied Cyril.

"That's not fair," grumbled Hazel.

"Conker had two goes and I didn't have any."

"Don't worry, Haze," said Conker, "it's not as much fun as it looks."

"You're just saying that to make me feel better."

Conker grinned. "Yeah, you're right," he admitted. "It was brilliant!"

The river was much deeper in this part of the woods. Although it was high summer, there had been thunderstorms during the previous week and water had tumbled down from hills and streams to fill the river bed.

"We could climb around it," said Daisy, pointing to a tree trunk that jutted out from the side of the bank.

"We could," considered Boom, focusing his gaze on something further downstream. "But we'd have to be very careful not to fall into *that*."

Beneath the branches of a weeping willow tree the river grew dark and spun around upon itself, like water disappearing down a plughole.

"What is it?" Daisy whispered.

"That," said Boom, "is Darkwater Sump."

Gripping tightly onto a branch that grew above the river, Daisy planted one foot firmly in the centre of the tree trunk and swung herself round until she hung suspended over the water.

"Steady now!" warned Boom. "Don't fall!"

"Don't worry!" Daisy called back. "I'm all right!"

Still hanging onto the branch, she walked herself around the tree trunk until she was almost at the other side, then pushed off with both feet and landed with a soft thump.

"Made it!" she exclaimed. She heard a faint pattering sound above her and looked up to see Hazel and Conker standing on the end of a branch, clapping their paws together.

"Well done, Daisy!" shouted Hazel. "You should have been a squirrel!"

Daisy glanced back at Boom and saw that he was looking worried. "Are you all right, Boom?"

"Ye–es," said Boom uncertainly. He looked up at the tree and then back at the river. "It's just … I don't know if I can swim."

Daisy realized that, although he was being brave, Boom was afraid of the fast-flowing water.

"Here," she said, catching hold of the branch again and swinging back to the middle of the tree trunk. "Let me help you."

She held onto the branch with one hand and stretched out the other towards Boom.

Boom took one last look at the water. Then, as he scrabbled at the bank, Daisy grabbed him by the collar and hauled him round to the other side.

"Yay!" cheered the squirrels as Daisy jumped down next to Boom and gave him a hug.

"Thanks for helping," he whispered.

Daisy pressed her cheek against his. "That's what friends are for," she said.

"Right," announced Cyril. "We are now nearing our objective, so I suggest we keep communication to a minimum."

"What's he on about?" asked Conker.

"I think he means we'd better keep quiet," Daisy explained. "He doesn't want us to frighten the otters."

"Oh. Why didn't he say so then?"

"Code, I expect," said Hazel, tapping her nose. "Top-secret code."

They walked along the path in silence for a while. In the treetops, a bird sang a song about storms.

"Look," said Boom. "I think we're nearly there."

Ahead of them, the woods opened out into a deep meadow. The grass was drenched with wild flowers: blue cornflowers and yellow buttercups jostled with pink campion and purple cranesbill. A breath of wind sent a wave of colour rippling across the surface like a whisper.

"Oh," breathed Daisy. "It's beautiful!"

On a bend in the river, beneath a line of willow trees, was a deep, shining pool.

In the middle of the pool, something moved.

"Is that them?" she whispered. "Is that the otters?"

"That's them all right," said Boom. "But I think they might be rather wary of you, Daisy. In the past, humans have destroyed their habitats. They've built houses, roads and factories in the places where otters used to live. Sometimes they've even hunted them."

"But that's terrible!" Daisy protested. "Why would anyone do that?"

"I suppose," said Hazel, sitting on Daisy's shoe and gazing up at her, "it's because not everyone is as nice as you."

Daisy stroked the little squirrel's head and looked at Cyril anxiously.

"Does that mean the otters won't want to see me?"

"Well," said Cyril, taking charge again, "there's only one way to find out."

Dampsy and Spray

When they reached the far side of the meadow, Daisy pushed her way through a curtain of willow branches and stood on the river bank, looking down into the deep pool. There was a flash of blue as a kingfisher flew across the surface before disappearing into a clump of trees. But there was no sign of the otters.

Cyril sat on a branch, swaying in the breeze. “Can’t see ’em,” he said. “How about you, Boom?”

Boom lifted his paw and Daisy saw that he was pointing to a raft of branches. Beyond it, two pairs of eyes stared out from a hole in the river bank.

"There they are!" whispered Hazel, hiding behind Daisy's leg. "Are they fierce?"

"No," Daisy reassured her, "but I expect they're a bit nervous. They don't know who we are."

"I'll go and have a word," said Cyril. He scampered down the tree and ran along the bank until he came to the pile of branches. Skipping nimbly over the top, he stood on a log that was half submerged in the water and peered into the otters' den. Although she couldn't hear what Cyril was saying,

Daisy could see that he was doing his best to explain the situation. Occasionally he would turn and point in their direction, and Daisy would see the brown eyes looking out at her, bright and unblinking. Then, all of a sudden, the two otters emerged from the safety of their hole and slid silently into the river. Daisy watched them glide beneath the surface as smoothly as swallows through the sky. Then they were scrambling up the bank towards her, their sleek brown coats shining in the sunlight.

"Hello," said the smallest otter. "You must be Daisy."

"Yes," said Daisy shyly. "It's lovely to meet you."

The otters turned to look at one another, then looked back at her again.

"So it's true," said the larger of the two. "You really can understand us!"

"Yes," said Daisy. "Does that seem strange?"

"Well, dear," said the smaller otter, "it's not every day we have a conversation with a real, live girl. Is it, Spray?"

"No," said Spray, and Daisy could tell that he was still a bit suspicious of her. "The world is full of surprises, missus."

"I'm Dampsy by the way," said the smaller otter, "and this is Spray." She winked at Daisy. "He'll cheer up once he realizes you're not going to steal his fish."

"It's not the fish I'm worried about," said Spray. "She's a human, isn't she? How do we know we can trust her?"

"Oh *really*, Spray!" Dampsy tutted and shook her head. "You've only got to look at her. You can see it in her eyes. She'd never hurt us in a million years!"

Spray studied Daisy for a moment and nodded. "Aye, she's a good'un, missus. But what if she tells the others where we are? They'll come with their big machines and that'll be the end of us."

"I won't tell anyone," promised Daisy. "I just want to take some pictures, that's all."

She took the camera from around her neck and showed them the pictures she had already taken.

Their eyes widened in disbelief as she showed them the photographs of Hazel and Conker playing in the water trough.

"I never knew such things existed!" gasped Dampsy. "Water squirrels, indeed!"

"Daft squirrels more like," muttered Cyril.

"Can you make pictures of us too?" asked Dampsy.

"Of course," said Daisy. "Perhaps I could take some over by your house. Would that be all right?"

"House?" Spray looked puzzled.

"She means our den," explained Dampsy. "Don't you, dear?"

"Can't see that it can hurt, missus. Follow me," said Spray. He slid back into the river and Dampsy joined him, disappearing beneath the surface with a plop.

"Well done, Daisy," said Boom as they watched the two otters swim back towards their den. "I think you've won them over."

"They weren't frightening at all," said Hazel, emerging from her hiding place behind Daisy's leg.

"Do you want to come, then?" asked Daisy.

Hazel stared at the ground for a moment as if trying to remember something she had forgotten. "Umm…" she said. "Ummm…"

"I wonder," said Boom in a kind voice, "if anyone will stay here and keep me company?"

"I will!" cried Hazel, sounding relieved. "If Daisy doesn't mind, that is."

Daisy smiled. "Of course not. You stay here with Boom. Cyril and Conker can collect some berries and I'll get a few pictures. Then we'll all have lunch. Does that sound like a good plan?"

"It does," said Cyril. "In fact, I was just on the point of suggesting it myself."

* * *

"Sorry about the mess," said Dampsy, sweeping some old fish heads beneath a branch with her paw. If I'd known you were coming I'd have cleaned up a bit."

"Don't worry," said Daisy. "It's a lovely den."

"Now then, young Daisy," said Spray. "Where would you like us?"

Daisy held up the camera. The two otters were framed in the viewfinder, with the entrance to the den behind them. "Hold it there!" she said, pressing the button. "You look great!"

After she had taken a few pictures of them in the water, the otters climbed out to see the results.

"Oh *my*!" exclaimed Dampsy. "Look, Spray, that's us. Swimming up and down in our own little pool!"

"That's a very fine job, Daisy," said Spray. "A very fine job indeed."

Daisy flushed pink with happiness.

"You must be hot and sticky after your journey," said Dampsy. "Why don't you come for a swim?"

Daisy looked down into the deep, clear water. It looked cool and inviting. "Really?" she asked. "Do you think I could?"

"Why not?" said Spray. "As the old saying goes, 'The day gets better as we all get wetter.'"

"I'll just check with the others," said Daisy. "Make sure they don't mind."

"We've got water, fish and good company," said Spray. "What's to mind?"

"Wheeeee!" yelled Conker, launching himself off a high branch and hugging his knees to his chest. He landed in the river with a loud smack, showering everyone with water.

"Nice bombing, young water squirrel," said Spray as Conker rose spluttering to the surface. "Excellent technique."

There was another splash as Hazel, who had quickly overcome her shyness, landed in the water next to him. Daisy could see her little paws scrabbling about on the river bed before she pushed herself off and broke through the surface with a high-pitched squeak. She paddled her way towards the shallows and began splashing water at Cyril, who was supervising from the bank.

Boom was stretched out on the grass, watching with amusement.

"Aren't you coming in?" called Daisy, standing waist deep in the cool, refreshing water.

Boom shook his head. "Someone needs to guard the sandwiches."

Dampsy popped her head out of the water and tapped Daisy on the arm. "Come and swim with us!"

"I'm not very good at swimming underwater," said Daisy.

"But it's easy," said Dampsy. "Just hold your breath, open your eyes and follow me."

"Well ... OK." Daisy had never opened her eyes underwater before, but now seemed like a good time to start.

She took a deep breath, flicked her feet up and tumbled beneath the surface, her hair streaming behind her in the water. Her eyes went blurry at first, but after a few seconds everything became clear. She could see the otters ahead of her, twisting through duckweed and snuffling under stones, turning every now and then to check that she was following.

Daisy pulled back her arms and kicked her feet, wriggling over fallen branches and touching the shiny pebbles that lay on the river bed beneath her. Soon she had caught up with them.

As Spray chased a stickleback downriver, Dampsy pointed to a water beetle paddling along the bottom. She swam down until her nose was almost touching it, formed her mouth into an O and then, with a puff of her cheeks, blew a silver bubble of air which enveloped the beetle before wobbling and shimmering up to the surface in a pool of light. This made Daisy laugh so much that she swallowed some water and had to swim up to the surface, chuckling and spluttering her way back to the bank.

* * *

"These are the best ever," said Boom, wolfing down a ham sandwich. "What did you do, Daisy, sprinkle them with magic?"

"French mustard actually," said Daisy. "Gives them that extra tang."

"Tang!" repeated Conker, flicking the back of Hazel's head. "You're it!"

"Doesn't count," said Hazel through a mouthful of elderberries. "Had my legs crossed."

"Since when was that the rule?"

"Since you started saying 'tang' and whacking me on the back of the head," replied Hazel.

"Oh," said Conker. "Fair enough."

"If I might interrupt for a moment," said Cyril, holding up a paw. "I think we can safely say that this has been mission accomplished. All agreed?"

"Absolutely," said Daisy, offering a crisp to Dampsy, who shook her head and patted her

tummy to show that she was full. "Thank you, Cyril. Thank you, everyone. I think this is going to be my best project ever!"

Dampsy leant in towards Daisy and said, "Do you think we could have another look at the picture-box before you go?"

"Of course," Daisy replied, switching on the camera.

"Look, Spray," said Dampsy, "we're trapped and smiling inside the little box. It's a miracle, that's what it is!"

“A miracle indeed, missus,” said Spray.

“Let’s take one last picture,” said Daisy. “Of all of us.”

She put the camera on an old tree stump, set it to automatic and then ran back to join the others.

As the shutter clicked, Dampsy said, “There now. One day you’ll look in this magic box and remember the time you swam with us in the river.”

“I won’t need to,” replied Daisy, “because today is a day I will never forget.”

Darkwater Sump

Daisy had been having such a lovely time that she had quite forgotten about the weather. But when she looked into the sky, she saw dark thunderclouds stacked overhead. The wind was picking up and the air smelled of rain.

"I hate to break up the party," said Boom, "but I think we should be heading back. There's a storm coming."

"Thank you so much for having us," said Daisy. "It's been a wonderful afternoon."

"Come back and see us," said Dampsy, patting Hazel's arm. "Spray will catch some extra fish to celebrate, won't you, dear?"

"That I will, missus," said Spray, ruffling the fur on top of Conker's head. "That I will."

There were damp hugs all round, and then Daisy was running back through the meadow with the others. She climbed the stile and jumped down into the shade of the trees just as the heavens opened and the rain began to fall.

"Stay close, small squirrels!" shouted Cyril as thick water droplets tore through the leaves and splashed down onto the woodland floor.

"The day gets better as we all get wetter!" sang Conker, echoing Spray's words as he danced his way along the winding path. But Daisy could see that Boom was worried.

"What is it?" she asked. "What's the matter?"

Boom shook himself, sending droplets of water pattering off into the undergrowth. "All this rain," he said softly, "will make the river angry."

Daisy stroked his head. "Don't worry, Boom. When we get to the tree trunk, I'll hold on tight and I won't let you go. OK?"

Boom nodded. "OK," he said.

When they reached the tree-crossing, Cyril gripped Hazel and Conker by the paws to make sure there would be no more shenanigans with the electric fence.

"Go on," he said. "Up you go."

As the squirrels scampered up the tree, Daisy looked down and saw that the water had already risen to the level of the bank. The river seemed moody and mysterious now, very different from how it had felt when they'd swum in it only minutes before.

Daisy pushed her hair out of her eyes, grabbed hold of the branch and swung out over the river. She wriggled round, her toes splashing the surface, and saw her reflection in the dark waters below. Then she thumped both feet against the tree trunk, grabbed Boom's collar and hauled him across to safety.

She jumped down next to him and did a little dance in the rain.

"We did it! We did it! We did it, Boom. We did it!"

Boom nodded his head in time with the rhythm, but Daisy could tell that his heart wasn't really in it. All he wanted was to be back in the old barn again, safe and warm and dry.

"OK, Boom," she laughed. "I've stopped dancing. We can go home now."

At that moment there was a little cry, followed by a faint splash. Daisy spun around and saw that Hazel had fallen from the tree and was trying desperately to swim towards the bank. But the current was too strong. It was pulling her down towards Darkwater Sump.

"Hazel!" cried Daisy, running towards the water's edge.

"Wait!" Boom barked.

Without stopping to think, Daisy kicked off her shoes and threw herself headlong into the river.

"No!" Boom howled. *"Noooo!"*

The water was cold and Daisy gasped as she swam forwards, desperate to reach Hazel before the current took her away. She looked frantically about, but there was no sign of Hazel, and the current was much stronger here than it had been in the otters' pool. Daisy felt herself being pulled towards the whirlpool that swirled beneath the weeping willows, and knew that it would drag her down into Darkwater Sump.

"Help!" she cried. "Help me, please!"

At that moment, a wet, bedraggled head appeared in the water next to her.

"Boom!" she gasped. *"Boom!"*

"Hang onto my neck,"
he instructed, "and don't let go."

Daisy did as she was told. As Boom swam back towards the bank she felt the powerful sweep of his paws, paddling against the current that had almost carried her away. When they scrambled back onto the bank again, Daisy remembered why she had jumped into the river in the first place.

"Hazel!" she called, turning to scan the river and the willows and the dark water beneath them. "Oh, Hazel, where *are* you?"

They all stared at the place where Hazel had been only a few moments before and Cyril shook his head, whispering, "It's all my fault. It's all my fault."

"No," said Daisy, close to tears. "It's not your fault, Cyril. It's no one's fault."

"Yes it is," replied Cyril miserably. "I said this mission was too dangerous. I told them they shouldn't come. But I gave in, didn't I? I gave in when I should have said no."

Cyril put his head in his paws and Conker started to cry. Daisy bit her lip and looked up at the sky. If only she'd listened to Meadowsweet's warning, or told someone at home about her plan. She hadn't thought carefully about how dangerous this day could be. They should never have come this far alone.

The storm was over now and the only sound was raindrops falling

from the leaves, pattering gently down onto the woodland floor.

"What will I tell her mother?" Cyril muttered. "Whatever will I tell her?"

"Tell her she needs some swimming lessons," said a gruff voice behind them. "And a sip of warm elderberry juice probably wouldn't go amiss either."

They all turned to see a wet and thoroughly miserable-looking squirrel shivering beneath the dripping branches of a beech tree. Standing next to her was Spray the otter.

Daisy's eyes widened and Boom's mouth dropped open in disbelief.

"Hazel!" cried everyone.

Cyril ran and scooped her up in his arms while Conker danced around shouting, "She's alive! Hazel's alive!" at the top of his voice.

"When she saw the storm coming," explained Spray, "Dampsy told me to swim up and check that you folks were all right. And" – here he nodded in Hazel's direction and winked at Daisy – "as usual, it looks like the missus was right."

Daisy's Picture

"Finished your project then?" asked Boom as they ambled down the lane on Monday morning.

"Yup," said Daisy, patting her satchel. "Mission accomplished, as Cyril would say."

Boom chuckled. "It was a good day after all, wasn't it?"

"The best," said Daisy.

They walked on in silence for a while. Then Daisy stopped. She tucked a stray wisp of hair behind her ear. "Boom," she said. "There's something I've been meaning to ask you."

"Oh yes?" said Boom. "And what might that be?"

Daisy looked at him thoughtfully. "Well, I don't mean to be rude or anything, but I sort of got the impression that you didn't like water very much. That you might even be a little bit scared of it. Is that true?"

"Yes," Boom admitted in a quiet voice. "I fell in the river once when I was a puppy. I nearly drowned. I've been scared of water ever since."

"But I don't understand," said Daisy. "In that case, how come you jumped in and saved me?"

Boom scratched at the ground with his paw and said nothing. In the distance, Daisy could hear the school bell ringing.

"Boom?" she asked again. "How come

you saved me if you were so scared?"

Boom stopped scratching and looked up at her shyly.

"Because," he said, "the thought of losing you scared me even more."

As Daisy hugged him and ran away towards the school gates, Boom thought about the picture that she'd printed off that morning. She'd asked Cyril to take it to the otters, to say thank you for a wonderful day and for giving Hazel her life back.

Walking back up the lane listening to the bees buzz lazily among the foxgloves, Boom thought of the men who would come to the river one day, arriving with their bulldozers to build factories, roads and houses.

He imagined them in years to come, digging up the earth and branches of an abandoned otters' den and scratching their heads as they looked down at an old, faded photograph.

A photograph of three squirrels, two otters and a dog.

And a little girl with wet hair and her arms around them all, smiling in the light of a summer's afternoon.

Steve Voake is the author of five novels for older readers including *The Dreamwalker's Child,* and also writes the Hooey Higgins series for Walker Books. This is his second Daisy Dawson book. He says, "My daughter Daisy loves animals, and when she was little, she was always having conversations with them. I imagined what it would be like if they started talking back to her – and that's how Daisy Dawson was born!"

Steve lives in Somerset.

Jessica Meserve is the author and illustrator of the picture books *Small, Can Anybody Hear Me?* and *Bedtime without Arthur.* She has illustrated several other titles including *Drawing Together* by Mimi Thebo, *Grandad and John* by Jeanne Willis and the previous Daisy Dawson books. She says, "As a girl I wished I could talk to animals too. I love illustrating Daisy because she lets me have those adventures as a grown-up."